ST REGINA'S
CLASS

Mrs Bottomley-Blunt

Headmistress.
Has a long, laminated List of Rules.
Makes a noise like a horse when
she is annoyed, which is a lot.

Mr Nidgett

Teacher of 4B.
Firm believer that
everything can be
mended with kindness.
Often proved wrong.

Stanley Bradshaw

Fond of footling, fiddle-faddling
and shilly-shallying, much to
Mrs Bottomley-Blunt's annoyance.

Manjit Morris

Stanley's best friend.
Determined to be the First Human
Boy ever to do a lot of dangerous,
foolish and impossible things.

Keith Mears

Self-proclaimed King of the Internet.
Falls asleep in class a lot.

PRIMARY

B

Lionel Dawes

Called Lionel, even though she is a girl, because her mum says names do not have genders, they are just words, which is true if you think about it, but Mrs Bottomley-Blunt does not agree.

Bruce Bingley

Once got a plastic brontosaurus stuck up his nose for a week. Can burp the national anthem.

Lacey Braithwaite

Compulsive liar.

Penelope Potts

Annoying telltale. Identical twin of Hermione Potts in 4A, and determined to join her by fair means or foul.

Muriel Lemon

Knows too many medical facts. Fond of warning Mr Nidgett of the dangers of everything.

Harvey Barlow

Eater of many biscuits. Often mistaken for a Year 6.

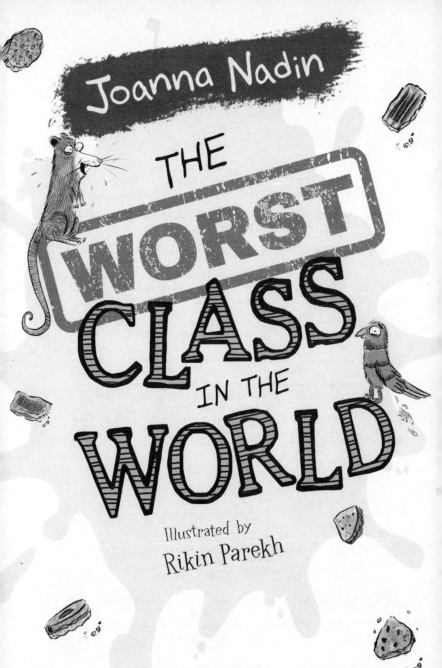

Joanna Nadin

THE
WORST
CLASS
IN THE
WORLD

Illustrated by
Rikin Parekh

BLOOMSBURY
CHILDREN'S BOOKS
LONDON   OXFORD   NEW YORK   NEW DELHI   SYDNEY

BLOOMSBURY CHILDREN'S BOOKS
Bloomsbury Publishing Plc
50 Bedford Square, London WC1B 3DP, UK

BLOOMSBURY, BLOOMSBURY CHILDREN'S BOOKS and the Diana logo
are trademarks of Bloomsbury Publishing Plc

First published in Great Britain in 2020 by Bloomsbury Publishing Plc

A catalogue record for this book is available from the British Library

ISBN: PB: 978-1-5266-1183-3; eBook: 978-1-5266-1185-7

2 4 6 8 10 9 7 5 3

Typeset by Tracey Cunnell

Printed and bound in Great Britain by CPI Group (UK) Ltd, Croydon CR0 4YY

To find out more about our authors and books visit www.bloomsbury.com
and sign up for our newsletters

In memory of my deputy headmaster, Mr Pett,
who was as terrifying to us as Mrs Bottomley-Blunt,
but also as kind as Mr Nidgett, as clever as Manjit
and as funny as Stanley

– J.N.

For the following teachers, who were THE best in
their individual, magical ways: Ms Wilson, Mrs Shah,
Señor Campos, Mr Meyer, Ms McGinn and Mr Alden.
A special BIG UP to Mrs Williams and Ms Bickle,
two of THE most eloquent teachers EVER!

– R.P.

Our class is the **WORST CLASS IN THE WORLD**.

I know it is the **WORST CLASS IN THE WORLD** because Mrs Bottomley-Blunt (who is our headmistress, and who makes

a noise like a horse when she is
annoyed, which is a lot) is always
taking our teacher into the corridor
and saying,

'Mr Nidgett, I have come across some rotten eggs in my time, but 4B is **LITERALLY** the **WORST CLASS IN THE WORLD**.'

LITERALLY means actually scientifically **TRUE**. Mrs Bottomley-Blunt pointed that out when Manjit Morris (who is my best friend, and who is going to be the First Human Boy to Swim Faster than a Shark) said his head had **LITERALLY** exploded when he got a dog called Killer for his birthday, and it actually hadn't.

It is true that a lot of things do not go as well as they could in class 4B. For example:

1. The time Penelope Potts became Playground Monitor and reported us all for trying to tunnel to Finland.

2. The time we went on a school trip to Grimley Zoo and Harvey Barlow smuggled a penguin back on the bus.

3. The time Manjit brought Killer in for Show and Tell and she ate four gel pens, Lacey Braithwaite's rubber that smells of strawberry and Mr Nidgett's Emergency Shoes.

Plus no one has won a prize all year, and 4A have won:

1. Best Assembly About Monkeys.
2. Best Being Silent when Mrs Bottomley-Blunt Bangs Her Gong.
3. Best Raffia Owl Display.

Although this is not surprising as their class captain is Eustace Troy, who is president of chess club, first violin in the school orchestra and team leader on the Shining Examples competitive spelling squad.

Our class captain is Bruce Bingley, who can only burp the national anthem, which I think is quite impressive, but Mrs Bottomley-Blunt does not.

BURP!!

She says school is not about footling or fiddle-faddling or **FUN**. It is about **LEARNING** and it is high time we tried harder to **EXCEL** at it.

Dad says well at least I haven't been arrested. Grandpa says being arrested would be getting off lightly and **IN HIS DAY** he had to walk five miles to school barefoot and eat gravel for lunch.

Mum, who works at the council, says, 'I have spent all day listening to Mr Butterworth bang on about bollards and the last thing I need is a heated debate about eating gravel. As long as Stanley's happy, that's all that matters.'

And you know what? I am happy, because:

1. According to Mr Nidgett, everyone excels at something, even Harvey Barlow – they just have to look very hard to find it.

2. According to the laws of probability, we have had all our bad luck and nothing else can possibly go wrong.

3. According to Manjit, even if it does

go wrong, we have a FOOLPROOF PLAN to get away with it, which is DO NOT TELL ANYONE.

You see, 4B may be the **WORST CLASS IN THE WORLD**. But I like it.

The Biscuit King

Lacey Braithwaite says it's Harvey
Barlow's fault for bringing in
discount biscuits.

Harvey Barlow says it's Manjit
Morris's fault for offering him a
broken yo-yo and a stone that

might be a dinosaur claw for a discount biscuit.

Manjit says it's Lacey Braithwaite's fault for claiming her biscuits are superior, and also for being so mean with her biscuits in the first place.

Mr Nidgett says he doesn't actually care whose fault it is as long as the Biscuit Madness is finished or he will **LITERALLY** resign from teaching and become a llama farmer because it cannot be harder than this.

I don't know whose fault it is, but I do know it started on Monday.

What happened was that Manjit and me were footling around at first break, up to nothing in particular, when Manjit saw Lacey Braithwaite hiding behind the Smelly Death Log, i.e. the hollow log with the bird poo on it, which no one even goes near unless they are up to **NO GOOD**. Not since Bruce Bingley claimed it had an ancient curse on it and if you touched the poo for more than a second you would be swallowed by The Ghost Pigeon.

Manjit said we should spy on Lacey and see what she was up to, because it was bound to be **SUSPICIOUS**. Which it totally was,

because when we got there, we saw that she had got a WHOLE packet of biscuits, which is against:

1. Mr Nidgett's Healthy Snacking guidelines (i.e. one piece of fruit or one nutritious biscuit), and

2. NO BEING GREEDY and NO SHOWING OFF, which are numbers 23 and 47 in Mrs Bottomley-Blunt's List of Rules (the actual List of Rules is laminated and stuck to her door and nothing can remove it, not even a metal ruler, which Manjit has tried) and

3. The curse of the Smelly Death Log.

So I said we should report her
to Mr Nidgett immediately so
he could put her name on the
Disappointing Day board and then
she would lose five minutes of
golden time and have to tidy paint
pots instead.

Only Manjit said actually he
was quite peckish, even though he
 had already

eaten his

banana and

also my

banana

(because he is in training to be the First Human Boy to Eat Ten Bananas in Ten Seconds) and that he quite fancied a biscuit, and Lacey would have to give us one each because otherwise we might report her. It was a **FOOLPROOF PLAN** so I agreed.

Only when we asked Lacey Braithwaite, she said, 'No way and anyway these biscuits are too fancy for you, because these are **SUPERIOR** biscuits, because the biscuit bit is made with butter

from the world's most expensive
cows and the jam in the middle is
made with strawberries picked by
highly trained monkeys.'

Manjit said that was a lie, and
Lacey said, 'Is not.'

And Manjit said, 'Is too.'
And Lacey said, 'Is not.'
And Manjit said, 'Is too.'

And it went on like that for **LITERALLY** a whole minute (which I know because Manjit timed it) until I said I wasn't actually sure I fancied biscuits that had had monkey fingers on and maybe we should just report her to Mr Nidgett after all.

Only Lacey Braithwaite said in that case we would also have to report Harvey Barlow, who was busy eating discount biscuits behind the Poo Wagon (which is not actually a wagon made of poo,

it is the temporary boys' toilets,

because Manjit broke the real ones,

but that's another story).

Then Manjit said actually he

had got biscuits on his mind now

and unless he had one soon he

wouldn't be able to concentrate in maths, and also he might **LITERALLY** die of low blood sugar and I might too because of not even having had **ONE** banana, so we should go and see Harvey Barlow because, even though his biscuits weren't baked with butter from expensive cows, they would taste better because of **KINDNESS**, which Mr Nidgett says makes everything sweeter. So I agreed.

Only when we got to the Poo Wagon, Harvey said we couldn't

have a biscuit each because he had only got one discount biscuit left so we would have to decide between us who got it.

Manjit said we could fight for it, and I said we could not because:

    1. NO FIGHTING is number 43 in Mrs Bottomley-Blunt's List of Rules.

    2. I would lose.

So Manjit said we could toss a coin for it instead. Then Harvey Barlow said if we had a coin we could in fact just buy the biscuit.

Only Manjit said he didn't

have an actual coin, he only had
a broken yo-yo and a stone that
could be a fossil of a dinosaur claw.

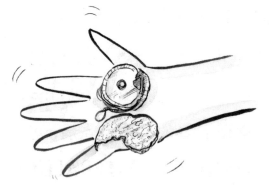

Then I said I had an actual coin
so maybe I could buy the biscuit,
and Harvey said yes. But then
Manjit said, 'But it's **LITERALLY**
possibly a dinosaur claw and also
I won't be able to concentrate in

maths and I might **LITERALLY** die of low blood sugar.'

But as the coin was **LITERALLY** ten pence Harvey said he could buy more biscuits with that and make an even bigger profit selling biscuits tomorrow, and then he would **LITERALLY** be the Biscuit King, so there.

Anyway, Manjit wasn't cross because:

1. I gave him half the biscuit, and

2. he came up with a FOOLPROOF PLAN in maths.

That plan was to become the Biscuit Kings ourselves, only we would make our own biscuits and they would be called Patented Manley Biscuits (which is our brand name and is half Manjit, half Stanley) and everyone would want to buy our biscuits and not Harvey Barlow's discount biscuits or even Lacey Braithwaite's monkey-finger ones. Also we would have **EXCELLED** at something so even Mrs Bottomley-Blunt would be pleased. And I said that was

definitely a **FOOLPROOF PLAN** and

we should do it tonight.

Which is when Lionel Dawes

(who is called Lionel even though

she is a girl, because her mum says

names do not have genders, they are just words, which is true if you think about it) heard us. She said, 'Do what tonight?'

So Manjit said, 'Make Manley Biscuits and sell them at break so we can **LITERALLY** become the Biscuit Kings of 4B.'

But Lionel said, 'Manly Biscuits do not sound nice at all and in fact I am going to make my own **NON-MANLY** biscuits and sell them to **SAVE THE WHALES**' (because she is very keen on saving whales and also polar bears and an endangered wasp, which everyone says would be better off dead, but Lionel does not agree – but that's another story) 'and they will be **SUPERIOR** because they are made with **CHEESE** and also **SEEDS** and then I will be the Biscuit King of 4B, only not King because that is sexist.'

Only Bruce Bingley overheard Lionel and he said, 'No one will buy your biscuits because they will smell of **CHEESY SEEDS** and also **WEIRDNESS** and in fact I am going

to make biscuits out of chocolate
and chewing gum, and everyone
will buy my biscuits and then I will
be the Biscuit King of 4B.'

But **HE** was overheard by Keith
Mears, who said he had seen a

recipe on the internet for biscuits
that could make you grow taller
or smaller and so he was going to
make that kind and then **HE** would
be Biscuit King of 4B.

Then Lacey Braithwaite said,

'You are all **DAFT** because the only biscuits worth buying are my monkey-finger biscuits and in fact I am bringing in two whole packets tomorrow and then you will all see.'

But Penelope Potts (who says it is not fair she is in 4B when her sister, Hermione, is in 4A) did not see. She said, 'If you don't all stop talking about biscuits I will report you to Mrs Bottomley-Blunt and **THEN** you will be sorry.'

Only Mr Nidgett overheard

that and said, 'Penelope Potts,
I am all for **EXTENDING YOUR
VOCABULARY** but could you also
get on with dividing two hundred
and thirty-eight by fourteen.'

So we said, 'Sorry, Mr Nidgett,' and did our dividing, and not a single one of us got it right, not even Penelope Potts.

But I didn't mind because after school we were going back to Manjit's to make our Manley Biscuits so we could be the Biscuit Kings of 4B.

Manjit's house is **OUTSTANDING**, because he is allowed to do all sorts of things that I am not. For example:

1. Try to be the First Human Boy to Dangle for an Hour off the Living-Room Door.

2. Try to be the First Human Boy to Invent Gold.

3. Make up recipes and cook them as long as his dad is at least in the same room, and he uses oven gloves, and doesn't try to melt the frying pan again.

So this is what we made:

MANLEY BISCUITS

by Manjit Morris and Stanley Bradshaw

INGREDIENTS:

Four eggs

Half a packet of flour

Half a packet of sugar

The butter that is left in the fridge

Some maple syrup or any other syrup that is left in the fridge

Some blue food colouring

Some green food colouring

Some red food colouring

Some yellow food colouring

Some black food colouring

Things to sprinkle on top, e.g. raisins or chocolate chips or anything small really

Jam or something squishy for sandwiching

METHOD:

Mix it all together then scoop it into biscuit-sized blobs and put on a tray. Bake until it just starts to burn then take out quickly using oven gloves and also a balaclava for added safety. When cold, sandwich together with squishy stuff as above.

I said I was not absolutely sure we had **EXCELLED** at making Manley Biscuits because:

1. All the different food colourings just made the mixture brown, which meant they looked chocolate flavour but were not, which might be disappointing.

2. The syrup wasn't maple syrup, it was Mr Morris's mentholated cough syrup (which he drinks straight from the bottle even though he does not have a cough. Although he says drinking it is WHY he doesn't have

a cough), which would definitely be
disappointing.

3. The jam for sandwiching was not
actually jam but in fact aubergine
chutney, which would definitely be
disappointing and also possibly
disgusting.

But Manjit said I was wrong,
because Manley Biscuits are
LITERALLY a special secret recipe
and so no one knows what they are
supposed to look like or taste like
and so they would be **NONE** the
wiser (even if they did look weird

and smell a bit of burned things, and also have hair in them from where Killer licked the bowl).

Mr Morris, who had done supervising from behind his newspaper, agreed.

So in the end I agreed too and said Manjit should be the one to bring them in tomorrow because:

    1. They were his idea.

    2. My grandpa might confiscate them
because he is keen on confiscating
things.

So the next day Manjit brought in the biscuits in a special box that he had decorated with War of the Wizards stickers and a sign that said: 'Manley Biscuits – 10p each'.

Lacey Braithwaite saw it and said, 'No one is going to pay ten pence for Manley Biscuits that smell of medicine, not when they can have two monkey-finger biscuits for the same price, and so I will win Battle of the Biscuits.'

Lionel Dawes said actually no one would pay ten pence for two monkey-finger biscuits when they could **SAVE THE WHALES** and also taste three of her nutritious **CHEESY SEEDY** biscuits for the same price and so **SHE** would win Battle of the Biscuits.

Keith Mears said his biscuits that could make you grow tall or small were four for ten pence (to make sure you were back to normal height at the end), and so **HE** would win Battle of the Biscuits.

Bruce Bingley said we were all wrong because his biscuits were five for ten pence and had a surprise prize in the middle, i.e. a piece of minty gum, so they would refresh your breath while you ate, which meant **HE** would win Battle of the Biscuits.

Harvey Barlow said his discount biscuits might not be minty but they were a whole packet for ten pence so HE would win Battle of the Biscuits.

Then Manjit said this was all our idea in the first place so WE

would win Battle of the Biscuits

and everyone else better shut

up or he would **LITERALLY**

spontaneously combust right there

and then (because he is very keen

on being the First Human Boy to

Spontaneously Combust).

Only he didn't because that's when Mr Nidgett came in and said he was all for **EXPANDING OUR MINDS** but could we also get on with drawing Henry the Eighth falling off a horse, which we did. But not before Manjit had passed round a note that said:

4B secret Battle of the Biscuits.
Meet at the Smelly Death Log
at first break.
Serious biscuit buyers only

So at break everyone trooped out
to the Smelly Death Log and set up
their stalls. And waited.

And waited.

And waited.

And then Manjit said, 'Why
isn't anyone buying biscuits?
Maybe you should buy a biscuit to
get them started, Stanley?'

But I said, 'I haven't got ten
pence, I've only got biscuits.'

Then Lacey Braithwaite said
she didn't have ten pence either.

And nor did Bruce Bingley, or

Keith Mears, or Lionel Dawes, or Harvey Barlow.

In fact no one had ten pence at all except Penelope Potts, and she said if we made her buy a biscuit she would report us to Mr Nidgett immediately and demand to be moved to 4A.

Then Lacey said, 'In that case we might as well **GIVE UP NOW** and agree that I am the Best Biscuit King of 4B.'

And Manjit said, 'But we don't know whose biscuits are

best until we taste them.'

And everyone nodded like mad.

And I said, 'Maybe we could just swap biscuits and taste them all and vote for our favouritist?'

Only Penelope Potts said we would just vote for our **OWN** biscuits, which would be **UNFAIR**, and in fact we needed an Impartial Biscuit Taster.

So I said maybe in fact **SHE** should be the Impartial Biscuit Taster, and everyone (except Lionel Dawes, who does not like Penelope because of an argument about peas in Year 1) agreed. And so she was.

First of all she ate one of Lacey Braithwaite's monkey-finger biscuits and gave it six points

for taste and crunch, with one point knocked off for the monkey jam tasting the same as normal strawberry.

Then she ate one of Lionel Dawes's savoury **CHEESY SEEDY**

SAVE THE WHALES biscuits and gave it ten points for taste and crunch, but deducted four points for having too many bits and for also being savoury, which meant it was a cracker not a biscuit.

Which Lionel said wasn't true and Penelope said, 'Is.'

And Lionel said, 'Is not.'

And Penelope said, 'Is.'

And Manjit said, 'Break is over in **LITERALLY** one minute so just get on with it!'

Which she did.

Next Penelope ate one of Keith Mears's Get Small and Tall biscuits and she did not get small or tall, which Manjit said was actually quite disappointing, and also they smelt a bit like a hamster cage, and Penelope agreed, and so they only got five points.

Then she ate one of Harvey

Barlow's discount biscuits and gave

it four points for crunch, six points

for taste and nine points for the

exciting extra, i.e. chocolate icing.

Only Harvey said it wasn't meant

to be an exciting extra, just that

he had been eating a chocolate-

spread sandwich in literacy and he

forgot to wash his hands, so she

took those points off again.

Then she ate one of Bruce

Bingley's chewing-gum biscuits

and gave it overall seven points

because there wasn't any gum

after all, only Bruce Bingley said

she must have swallowed it,

which meant her insides would be stuck together for **EVER**, and Keith Mears agreed because he had seen it on the internet. But Penelope said in that case they were both disqualified and it was only the Manley Biscuits left to test.

She was just about to put a Manley Biscuit in her mouth when Mrs Bottomley-Blunt stuck her head out of the office window and shouted, 'Who is lurking by the hollow log? Show yourselves at once!'

And Manjit said, 'We are

LITERALLY dead now.'

And I said, 'We're not, we just

have to **EAT** the evidence.'

And everyone agreed, even

Penelope Potts.

And so we did, and then
we showed ourselves, and Mrs
Bottomley-Blunt said, 'You are
LITERALLY the **WORST CLASS IN**

THE WORLD,' and put us all on Mr

Nidgett's Disappointing Day board

and sent us inside to tidy paint pots.

But it wasn't over yet.

The first one to be
sick was Penelope
Potts, who did it
in the sink.

Next was Bruce
Bingley, who did
it in a bucket.

Keith Mears
was sick in
the fish tank.

Then Lacey Braithwaite was sick in her book bag.

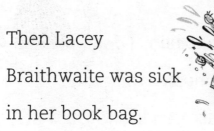

And Harvey Barlow was sick on Mr Nidgett's shoes and he had to change into his emergency ones again.

Mr Nidgett said, 'I do hope you haven't been eating mud again because you know full well it is against rule eleven in Mrs Bottomley-Blunt's list.'

Lacey Braithwaite said we hadn't.

Harvey Barlow said we hadn't.

Penelope Potts said we hadn't, and she never lies so Mr Nidgett said in that case what had we been eating?

Penelope said, 'Seventy-eight biscuits. I counted.'

Mr Nidgett sighed and said,
'And whose bright idea was that?'

And that's when everyone
argued and Mr Nidgett said he
was going to give up teaching and
become a llama farmer. Only we
didn't want that to happen or we

would get Mrs Bottomley-Blunt or worse, a **SUPPLY TEACHER**.

So Manjit said, 'It was only to see who was the Biscuit King of 4B and also because otherwise we might have **LITERALLY** died of low blood sugar.'

Mr Nidgett said, 'I'm not sure it's actually possible to **LITERALLY** die of low blood sugar, Manjit.'

But Muriel Lemon, whose parents are both doctors and who is excused from all dangerous activities, e.g. netball, football and science experiments, said, 'Actually you can die of low blood sugar, it is called hypoglycaemia.'

Then Lionel Dawes said, 'And also not eating the biscuits would have been a waste and what would the starving orphans think?'

Mr Nidgett is very keen on orphans and them not starving, and also on no one dying in class, so he said in that case he could understand why we did it, but to please not do it again, and also he would have to send anyone who was sick home with a note from Mrs Bottomley-Blunt.

And that's when Manjit realised something, i.e. me and him hadn't been sick at all.

Harvey Barlow said, 'It's a miracle.'

I said, 'It's a mystery.'

But Manjit said, 'No, it's Manley Biscuits!'

And I said, 'What?'

Then he said we had only eaten our own biscuits when we were getting rid of the evidence and so they must have been **SUPERIOR** after all, and so in fact we were **LITERALLY** the Biscuit Kings of 4B and so we had **DEFINITELY EXCELLED** at something. And I agreed and it felt **OUTSTANDING**.

But not for long.

Because Mrs Bottomley-Blunt was not at all happy about the sick, or the biscuits. She took Mr Nidgett into the corridor and said, '4B is **LITERALLY** the **WORST CLASS IN THE WORLD**.' And Mr Nidgett could not disagree because 4A had just won Best Animal Made of Pasta.

When I got home, Grandpa said, 'Why do you smell of sick and cough syrup, Stanley Bradshaw?

You had better not have been up to **NO GOOD** with That Manjit again.'

I said I had definitely not been, and the smell was just biscuits.

Dad said, 'Ooh, I love a biscuit.'

Grandpa said, '**IN MY DAY** we didn't even have biscuits. We had to eat salty **CARDBOARD** and be glad about it.'

Mum said, 'I've just spent three hours listening to Mr Butterworth bang on about paper clips and the last thing I need is a heated debate about salty cardboard. As long

as Stanley's happy that's all that
matters.'

And you know what? I am.

Show and Tell

Penelope Potts says it's Bruce
Bingley's fault for bringing in his
rat called Fingers to Show and Tell.

Bruce Bingley says it's Manjit
Morris's fault for bringing in his
dog called Killer to Show and Tell.

Manjit says it's Harvey Barlow's fault for only bringing in crisps to Show and Tell, which is why they brought Fingers and Killer in in the first place.

Mr Nidgett says he doesn't actually care whose fault it is as long as the Show and Tell madness is finished or he will **LITERALLY**

resign from teaching and become a lion tamer because it cannot be harder than this.

I don't know whose fault it is, but I do know it started on Wednesday.

Every Wednesday it is Show and Tell. Which is:

1. My Second Best Thing About School (after chocolate sponge pudding on a Friday) because it means we don't have to do maths that morning.

2. Manjit's Third Best Thing About

School (after chocolate sponge for pudding on a Friday and the newt pond) because he gets to try to be the First Human Boy to Do Something OUTSTANDING, e.g. juggle an apple, a sock and a book about bees. It doesn't always go to plan but Mr Nidgett says it is the TRYING that counts and Manjit is LITERALLY the best tryer in the world.

3. The Bane of Mr Nidgett's Life, which means it is his Absolutely Worst Thing About School, because it always involves Mrs Bottomley–Blunt

swooping in for a Surprise Inspection
and telling us we are the WORST CLASS
IN THE WORLD because nothing we are
showing and telling is Interesting or
Informative or as OUTSTANDING as 4A.
It is just mainly messy.

On this Wednesday what happened
was Manjit had just finished trying
to be the First Human Boy to Drink
a Cup of Milk While Blindfolded and
Spinning Around Without Spilling a
Drop (which he didn't, he spilt it all
over Mr Nidgett's Emergency Shoes,

which he was already wearing because of an Incident with Some Paint, and so he had to just wear socks) and next it was Harvey Barlow's turn.

Lacey Braithwaite said, 'I bet he has got crisps, it is **ALWAYS** crisps.'

And Manjit said, 'That is a **TOTAL LIE**, once it was a jam tart.'

 And Lacey said, 'Wasn't.'

And Manjit said, 'Was.'

And Lacey said, 'Wasn't.'

And it turned out Lacey was right because the jam tart had just been a random snack, and this time Harvey had brought in a packet of crisps after all.

But Mr Nidgett didn't mind.

He said, 'I have told you before,

the point of Show and Tell is

that we all find different things

interesting and if Harvey finds crisps interesting then that's all that matters, so please pipe down and let him get on with it.'

So we did all pipe down and let Harvey get on with it and he told us that he had found a prawn cocktail crisp in a packet that was actually supposed to be salt and vinegar, which he said was interesting but also annoying.

Lionel Dawes said it was actually **TERRIFYING**, because she does not eat anything with a face.

Manjit said he actually might have **LITERALLY** died because he is allergic to prawns.

Mr Nidgett said no one was

likely to **LITERALLY** die from a packet of crisps, not even prawn cocktail, because there is no actual prawn in them just the smell.

But Muriel Lemon, whose parents are both doctors, and who is excused from all dangerous activities, e.g. netball, football and science experiments, said, 'Actually you can die from crisps, because you can choke on them.' Which is when Mrs Bottomley-Blunt swooped in for a **SURPRISE INSPECTION**.

She said, 'Harvey Barlow, is that a packet of crisps you are eating when it is neither breaktime nor lunchtime because that is against rule nine, as well you know?'

Harvey said no it wasn't. Mrs Bottomley-Blunt made a noise like a horse and said, 'And lying is against rule one hundred and two.'

But Manjit said Harvey wasn't lying because it wasn't a packet of crisps at that actual second in time, it was his Show and Tell exhibit, and it was **LITERALLY** terrifying and he had **LITERALLY** nearly died, so it was **LITERALLY** within school rules. And everyone agreed, except Mrs Bottomley-Blunt.

She said, 'I am reaching the end of my tether, Mr Nidgett. If I've told you once, I've told you a hundred times, things like crisps are neither Informative, Interesting nor **OUTSTANDING**. It is high time this class took a leaf out of 4A's

book when it comes to Show and Tell, because there is not a crisp in sight, nor is their floor covered in milk, and their teacher, Major Wellington, is always wearing actual shoes and not just socks with cats on.'

Mr Nidgett started to explain about Manjit being the First Human Boy to Drink a Cup of Milk While Spinning but Mrs Bottomley-Blunt said she had heard quite enough, and tomorrow there would now be a Grand Show and Tell during assembly against 4A and we had better Up Our Game because whoever won would get a prize.

Everyone went 'ooh!' at that. But Lacey Braithwaite said, 'What sort of prize? Is it the Joy of Winning again?'

Because Mrs Bottomley-Blunt hardly ever gives prizes except for the Joy of Winning, which is not really a prize when you think about it.

Mrs Bottomley-Blunt said, 'It shouldn't matter what the prize is, or even if there is no prize at all.'

Then Penelope Potts said, 'But you said there was a prize, so is there a prize or isn't there?'

So Mrs Bottomley-Blunt said, 'Oh for heaven's sake, yes,' and then swooped out again to tell

Mrs Pickens (who is the school secretary, and who smells of soup) to fetch the mop.

Which meant everyone was immediately **MAD** with excitement guessing what the prize might be.

Penelope Potts said it might be a place in class 4A, and she should get it because her sister is already there and that is **UNFAIR**.

Only Keith Mears said that wouldn't work because why would anyone in 4A want to win a place in their own class, which everyone agreed was **WEIRD**.

Bruce Bingley said it might be a trophy made of actual gold, which would be brilliant because then he could sell it on the internet for **THOUSANDS** of pounds.

Manjit said it might be a War of the Wizards helmet made of actual invisibility, which would be brilliant because then he could sell it on the internet for **LITERALLY MILLIONS** of pounds. Only Keith Mears said that would mean Mrs Bottomley-Blunt would have to

have had millions of pounds to
buy one in the first place. So then
everyone started arguing about
how much War of the Wizards
helmets cost, and if they are
invisible how can you even tell
if you have one, and how much
money Mrs Bottomley-Blunt even

has anyway, which is when Mr Nidgett said perhaps we had better use our time more **WISELY**, i.e. to decide what **OUTSTANDING** thing to bring in for Show and Tell first or none of us would be winning any prizes at all.

Lacey Braithwaite said she was going to bring in a real live skeleton of her dead hamster, Mabel, who had had one red eye and one black eye, which is highly **OUTSTANDING**. Only Bruce Bingley said that wasn't

OUTSTANDING enough to win unless Mabel also had e.g. five legs, and Lacey said actually she had so there.

So Bruce Bingley said he was going to bring in his real live rat,

Fingers, who is **OUTSTANDING** because he has laser eyes that can kill a hamster at twenty paces.

Only Lionel Dawes said he shouldn't bring in Fingers because No Pets is number 103 in Mrs Bottomley-Blunt's List of Rules.

Only Bruce said Fingers wasn't a pet, he was a **WORKING ANIMAL**, because he eats flies, which is useful, and working animals are exempt from all laws, and Manjit, whose mum is a police officer, said it was true.

Then Lionel Dawes said in that case she was going to bring in her cat Dave (which is called Dave

even though it is a girl, because
her mum says names do not have
genders, they are just words,
which is true if you think about it)
and she is also a working animal
because she will eat Fingers, which
is useful.

So Manjit said in that case he
was going to bring in his dog Killer,
who is also a working animal
because she is half police dog and
can do amazing tricks and also
she will eat Dave and Fingers and
probably the real live skeleton of
dead Mabel too.

Which is when Mr Nidgett said
perhaps we could decide what
to bring in later and get back to
working out what a semicolon was
for instead. Which we did, and no
one got it right, not even Penelope
Potts. But I didn't care because
I was too busy worrying what I
could bring in for Show and Tell
that would be **OUTSTANDING** and
better than Killer eating everyone.

But I needn't have worried because
after school Manjit came up with

a **FOOLPROOF PLAN**, which was to go to the shop on the corner, which is called Paradise City, and which has a sign on the window that says:

We Sell Everything

Then I would be able to buy something **OUTSTANDING** with the forty-seven pence I had in my pocket. So we did.

Only it turns out that Paradise
City doesn't actually sell any of the
OUTSTANDING things I wanted, e.g.:

1. Night-vision swimming goggles.
2. Antique ski poles.
3. A stuffed monkey holding an orange.
4. Live snakes.
5. Dead dinosaur eggs.
6. A piece of moon in a box.
7. A plum with a maggot in.
8. A gold-plated toilet brush.
9. A scale model of a combustion
engine.
10. The Emperor of Zarg

Which Manjit said was **FALSE ADVERTISING**, but Mrs Beasley (who is in charge of Paradise City and whose eyebrows meet in the middle, which Manjit says means she is a werewolf) said if we didn't stop being **EEJITS** and actually buy something then we would be **BARRED FOR LIFE**.

And Manjit said, 'But not **LITERALLY** life.'

And she said, 'Yes, **LITERALLY** until you are dead.'

And so we stopped and bought

two chocolate frogs and ate them

while we thought up plan B, which

was to go home and find some

OUTSTANDING things there instead.

When we got home, we searched
the whole house for something
OUTSTANDING.

In my bedroom we found:

1. Eighty-four War of the Wizards
cards.

2. A dead spider.

3. A robot with a broken arm.

But none of them seemed
OUTSTANDING enough to win
Show and Tell.

In the kitchen we found:

1. A tin whose label had fallen off so no one dared open it in case it was mandarins, because no one likes them.

2. A spatula that was a bit bent.

3. And some cheese that was a month past its use-by date.

Grandpa said that was nothing and **IN HIS DAY** they ate cheese that was fourteen years past its use-by date and they had lived to tell the tale.

Then he said I should in fact take **HIM** in for Show and Tell because he is a walking **MIRACLE** because he has survived two world wars as well as the out-of-date cheese.

Only Mum said no, he is not a walking **MIRACLE**, because in fact he wasn't born until the wars were all over and eating mouldy cheese is not something to be proud of and perhaps I should just take the broken robot in instead.

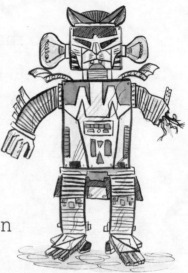

Which is when Manjit had his idea for plan C, which was that I could be part of his act with Killer, i.e. he would be in charge and I could do a daring trick with her, e.g. put my whole head in her mouth, and it would be the

Amazing Manley Animal Show (which is our brand name and is half Manjit and half Stanley). So I agreed. And so did Mum, except for putting my whole head in Killer's mouth, which she said was dangerous as well as unhygienic, as Killer likes to drink out of the toilet.

But Manjit said we would just do **UNDANGEROUS** tricks and could go and practise at his now, and it would **LITERALLY** be the easiest thing ever. So we did.

When we got to Manjit's house, it was not **LITERALLY** the easiest thing ever because Killer did not seem keen to do any tricks, i.e. when Manjit told her to lie down she just put her paws on his shoulders and licked his face, and when he told her to play dead she chewed a bit of the wall, and when he said 'sit' she just wandered off and ate a sock.

I said maybe I should show her what to do first, and Manjit

said that was very clever and also **FOOLPROOF**. So when Manjit said 'sit' I sat down. And then Killer did sit, but only on my lap and she also chewed a button off my shirt, which was not part of the plan.

Manjit said this is why she is only half a police dog and not a whole one, i.e. she is not very good at obeying orders or doing anything like not eating things she shouldn't. Which is true, because by the time we had given up training she had also eaten:

1. A pair of Manjit's pants.

2. Mr Morris's cough medicine (which he drinks even though he does not have a cough).

3. The TV remote, which was Highly Annoying because the telly was stuck

on a programme about worms and it
meant Mr Morris couldn't watch his
favourite quiz show and we couldn't
watch War of the
Wizards.

But Mr Morris said the trick could
in fact be Killer sitting on my lap
while eating things and Manjit
agreed and said it was **FOOLPROOF**
and it would be the best Amazing
Manley Animal Show ever and also
OUTSTANDING. Since we didn't
have a plan D and it was time to go
home for tea, I agreed.

And it was **OUTSTANDING** and **FOOLPROOF** because when we got to school the next day, Lionel Dawes hadn't brought Dave in after all. She said her mum had decided she didn't want Dave eating rats because she is a vegetarian cat and so she can't eat anything with a face either, so instead she had brought in a banana that was almost exactly straight.

Lacey Braithwaite hadn't brought
in the five-legged real live skeleton
of dead Mabel either. She said
she couldn't find it, and it was a
complete mystery, and probably
even ghosts were involved, so
instead she had brought in four gel
pens and a rubber that smells of
strawberry.

But Bruce
Bingley **HAD**
brought in Fingers,
and he was sitting
on Bruce's shoulder,
eating a bit of apple.

Although Manjit didn't care.
He said, 'That's nothing. Killer can
LITERALLY stand on Stanley's
shoulder and eat a whole **BAG** of
apples.'

And Bruce said, 'Well, Fingers
can sit on my **HEAD** and eat a
whole **DESK**.'

And Manjit said, 'Well, Killer can sit on Mrs Bottomley-Blunt's **BRAIN** and eat **HER**.'

Which is when Mr Nidgett walked in and said, 'Why in the name of all that is sacred is there a **DOG** in this classroom?'

And Bruce said, 'Never mind the **DOG**. I've got a rat than can kill you with his laser eyes from twenty paces!'

And Mr Nidgett said, 'For once in my life I actually hope you're lying.'

And Bruce said, 'Am not.'

And Manjit said, 'Are too.'

And Bruce said, 'Am not.'

And Manjit said, 'Are too.'

And Mr Nidgett said, 'Bruce Bingley, if you really have a rat, even one that does not have laser eyes, then you need to hand it over immediately before Mrs Bottomley-Blunt finds out.'

Only Bruce couldn't hand him over, because that's when we realised that Fingers had disappeared.

Everyone went 'ooh!' at that, except Penelope, who is scared of rats, and who started screaming, and except Bruce, who said if we didn't find Fingers immediately, then he would sue the school for damages, which would be

MILLIONS of pounds because Fingers was such a special rat.

Mr Nidgett said, 'I don't think any rat is that special.'

But Muriel Lemon said, 'Actually some rats can be trained to sniff out landmines, bombs and also tuberculosis so they are very special.'

Which is when Manjit said, 'Killer is half police dog and so she is trained to sniff out criminals and other missing things so she can sniff out Fingers and then you can

PAY me **MILLIONS** of pounds.'

But Bruce said he could only give him two toffees and a plastic monkey, and Manjit said fine.

Then I had a brilliant idea, which was to let Killer sniff Fingers's cardboard box to get his scent, which Mr Nidgett said was actually quite clever and so we did, and Killer only ate a bit of the box, which Manjit said was progress, and then we said 'Find Fingers!'

and let go of Killer, and off she went
around the classroom.

First she ate Lionel Dawes's
banana that was almost exactly
straight, so Lionel started screaming.

Next she ate Lacey
Braithwaite's four gel pens and the
rubber that smells of strawberry,
so Lacey started screaming.

Then she ate Mr Nidgett's
Emergency Shoes, which were

only just dry from all the milk
from yesterday, and he didn't
scream but he did say he was very
seriously thinking of becoming a
lion tamer because it cannot be
harder than this.

Only it could. Because that
was when Mrs Bottomley-Blunt
swooped in to ask why we were
causing such a kerfuffle when we
should have been in assembly
looking neat and obedient and
ready for the Grand Show and Tell.

And I could tell she was just

about to make a noise like a horse because she had seen Killer (who was still eating an Emergency Shoe), when something ran up her leg and climbed on to her shoulder and it was Fingers!

Everyone did a cheer, except Mrs Bottomley-Blunt, who grabbed him round the middle and didn't bother even going into the corridor before she said, 'Mr Nidgett, I have come across some rotten eggs in my time but 4B is **LITERALLY** the **WORST CLASS IN THE WORLD**.'

Then she banned our class from Show and Tell until we could be trusted not to bring in wild animals. Manjit started to explain about them being working animals but she said, 'Any more hoo-ha from any of you and you will be tidying paint pots **UNTIL KINGDOM COME**.'

Then she confiscated Fingers and Killer and locked them in her office until Bruce and Manjit's parents came to collect them.

Which is when everyone

started arguing again until Mr
Nidgett said we weren't actually
the **WORST CLASS IN THE
WORLD**, we were just a bit **TRYING**
at times.

And Manjit said, 'But you said it
is the **TRYING** that counts.'

And Mr Nidgett laughed and said so he had, and in that case perhaps we could **TRY** hard not to get into any bother for the rest of the day.

And we almost did.

When I got home, Grandpa said, 'Did you win Show and Tell with That Manjit and your idiotic dog tricks then?'

And I said, no. Because Eustace Troy won with a bit of the moon in a box.

Dad said, 'Oh, I love a dog trick.'

Grandpa said, '**IN MY DAY** we didn't even have dogs, we had bits of **WOOD** on **STRING** and were glad about it.'

Mum said, 'I've just spent all day listening to Mr Butterworth bang on about roundabouts and the last thing I need is a heated debate about bits of wood on string. As long as Stanley's happy, that's all that matters.'

And you know what? I am.

Because the prize was only the Joy of Winning after all.

And also Killer ate Mrs Bottomley-Blunt's laminated List of Rules.

Mrs Bottomley-Blunt's List of Rules

1. No running in the corridors.

2. No sliding in the corridors.

3. No playing ludo in the corridors.

4. No outside voices inside.

5. No outside voices outside.

6. No putting paper in plugholes to see if it will block them.

7. No putting anything down the toilet.

8. Especially no putting PE kit down the toilet.

9. No eating in class.

10. No eating in the corridors.

11. No eating mud anywhere.

12. No claiming you will eat the class hamster.

13. No claiming you are secretly royal.

14. No claiming you are actually dead.

15. No claiming Major Wellington is a vampire.

16. No hats.

17. No badges.

18. No yo-yos.

19. No fake swords.

20. No real swords.

21. No wearing a colander on your
    head instead of a hat.

22. No being rude.

23. No being greedy.

24. No being too clever by half.

25. No War of the Wizards cards.

26. No War of the Wizards cloaks.

27. No War of the Wizards wands.

28. No ketchup.

Wizard hats are NOT uniform

29. No frogs in jars.

30. No frogspawn in jars

31. No claiming sago pudding is frogspawn.

32. No claiming bubble tea is frogspawn.

33. No claiming anything is frogspawn.

34. No pretending to be deaf.

35. No pretending to be daft.

36. No being daft.

37. No hitting each other.

38. No pinching each other.

39. No biting each other.

4B Zoo Trip
October 11th
(WARN ZOO)

40. No poking each other.

41. No twisting anyone's ears.

42. No pulling anyone's hair.

43. No fighting in general.

44. No kerfuffle.

45. No shenanigans.

46. No tomfoolery.

47. No showing off.

48. No footling.

49. No fiddle-faddling.

50. No shilly-shallying.

Shopping

Rubbers
Soap
A loud bell
A mop
Ear plugs

N.U.T.

Mrs. Bottomley-Blunt
Head Teacher
ID#AUG2ND1979

Could
you be in

THE

WORST

CLASS

IN THE

WORLD?

Turn over and take
a fun quiz to find out!

1. If someone gave you a biscuit at breaktime, would you eat it?
YES or NO

2. Have you ever made your own biscuits to sell at school?
YES or NO

3. Have you ever been sick at school from eating too many biscuits?
YES or NO

4. If your favourite food was crisps, would you bring them in for Show and Tell?
YES or NO

5. If you had a banana that was almost exactly straight, would you bring it in for Show and Tell?
YES or NO

6. Would you bring your pet into school even if it wasn't allowed?
YES or NO

ANSWERS

Mostly YES – You could absolutely be one of the Worst Class in the World! Come and join in the fun!

Mostly NO – Sorry, you're probably more suited to being in Class 4A, but you can definitely still play with 4B at breaktime!

Which member of

THE

WORST

CLASS

IN THE

WORLD

should be your best friend?

Turn over and take
a fun quiz to find out!

1. What is your favourite thing?
a) Saving animals
b) Food
c) War of the Wizards

2. What do you do if you get into trouble?
a) Protest my innocence!
b) Eat a bag of crisps to feel better
c) Come up with a FOOLPROOF PLAN
to get away with it

3. What do you want to be when you
grow up?
a) An animal rights campaigner
b) A chef
c) The first human boy to break every
world record!

4. What is the best thing about school?
a) Being yourself
b) School dinners
c) Chocolate sponge pudding on Friday

ANSWERS

Mostly a –
Your best friend should be Lionel Dawes

Mostly b –
Your best friend should be Harvey Barlow

Mostly c –
Your best friend should be Manjit Morris

Joanna Nadin is an award-winning author who has written more than eighty books for children. She has also been a juggler, a lifeguard and an adviser to the Prime Minister. The worst thing she ever did at school was be sick on her plate at lunch and blame it on someone else. She lives in Bath and her favourite things are goats, monkeys and crisps.

Rikin Parekh (aka Mr Rik) is an author/illustrator and ninja. He also works in primary schools as an LSA and worked as a bookseller (which was REALLY, REALLY fun!). The worst thing he ever did at school was to draw all over his exercise books (and in the margins!) and then get a big telling off for it! He lives in Wembley and his favourite things are pizza, dogs, and picking his nose and collecting the bogeys.

LOOK OUT FOR MORE
HILARIOUS HIGH JINKS WHEN

THE
WORST
CLASS
IN THE
WORLD

GET WORSE

COMING SOON!